I0803724

ZOO CLUES 2

My Mane Is Short and Spiky

by Jessica Rudolph

Consultant:
Christopher Kuhar, PhD
Executive Director
Cleveland Metroparks Zoo
Cleveland, Ohio

BEARPORT PUBLISHING

New York, New York

Credits
Cover, © Peter Betts/Shutterstock; 4–5, © dangdumrong/Shutterstock; 6–7, © Enrique Ramos/Shutterstock; 8–9, © Antonio Jorge Nunes/Shutterstock; 10–11, © Alta Oosthuizen/Shutterstock; 12–13, © TTphoto/Shutterstock; 14–15, © Suzi Eszterhas/Minden Pictures; 16–17, © Peter Betts/Shutterstock; 18–19, © Prisma Bildagentur AG/Alamy Stock Photo; 20–21, © Prisma Bildagentur AG/Alamy Stock Photo; 22, © Dave Pusey/Shutterstock; 23, © Iakov Filimonov/Shutterstock; 24, © Iakov Filimonov/Shutterstock.

Publisher: Kenn Goin
Editor: J. Clark
Creative Director: Spencer Brinker
Design: Debrah Kaiser

Library of Congress Cataloging-in-Publication Data in process at time of publication (2017)
Library of Congress Control Number: 2016007668
ISBN-13: 978-1-944102-58-6

Copyright © 2017 Bearport Publishing Company, Inc. All rights reserved. No part of this publication may be reproduced in whole or in part, stored in any retrieval system, or transmitted in any form or by any means, electronic, mechanical, photocopying, recording, or otherwise, without written permission from the publisher.

For more information, write to Bearport Publishing Company, Inc., 45 West 21st Street, Suite 3B, New York, New York 10010. Printed in the United States of America.

10 9 8 7 6 5 4 3 2 1

Contents

What Am I?

Look at my ears.

They are big and round.

My fur is thick.

It has dark spots.

I have four legs.

They are very strong.

The bottoms of my paws are rough.

My tail
is black.

It is bushy, too.

I have big teeth.

They are white
and sharp.

My mane is
short and spiky.

What am I?

Let's find out!

I am a
spotted hyena!

Animal Facts

Spotted hyenas may look like dogs, but they are more closely related to cats. Like almost all mammals, hyenas give birth to live young that drink milk.

More Spotted Hyena Facts

Food:	Insects, birds, lizards, snakes, wildebeests, and antelopes
Size:	Up to 6 feet (1.8 m) long, including the tail
Weight:	Up to 190 pounds (86 kg)
Life Span:	About 25 years in the wild
Cool Fact:	Hyenas live in large groups and make many sounds to communicate. One noise they make sounds like a human laughing.

Adult Spotted Hyena Size

Where Do I Live?

Spotted hyenas live in grassy areas in Africa.

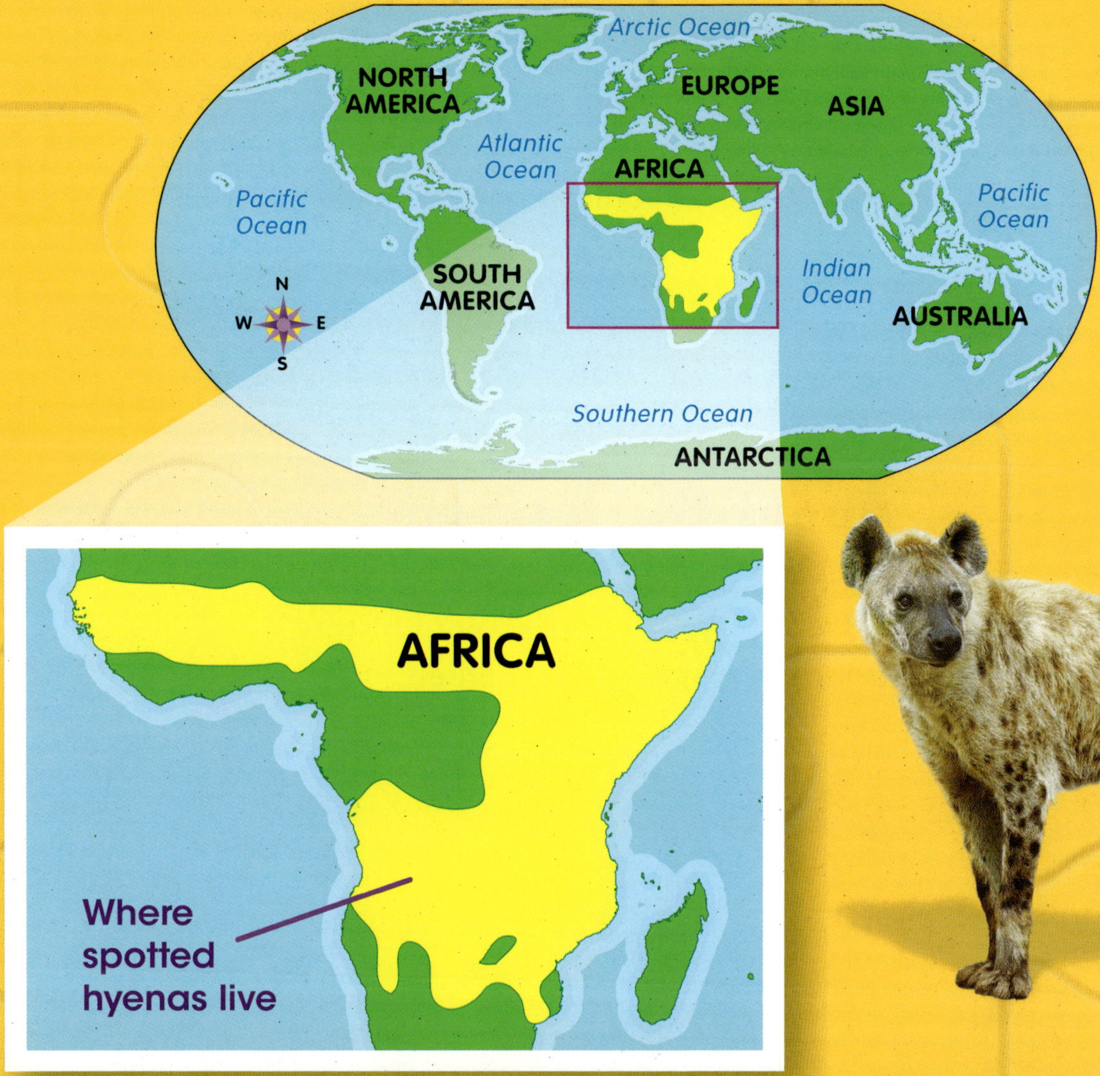

Index

Read More

Malam, John. *Hyenas (Scary Creatures).* New York: Franklin Watts (2009).

Spilsbury, Louise. *Hyena (A Day in the Life: Grassland Animals).* Chicago: Heinemann (2011).

Learn More Online

To learn more about spotted hyenas, visit
www.bearportpublishing.com/ZooClues

About the Author

Jessica Rudolph lives in Connecticut. She has edited and written many books about history, science, and nature for children.